A Far Out ASSIGNMENT

by Kate Boehm Jerome

sundance™ Newbridge®

sundance **Newbridge**

Program written and developed by Kate Boehm Jerome
in association with Sundance Newbridge Publishing.

Editorial, Design, and Production by Baseline Development Group
in association with Sundance Publishing.

Content reviewer: Rebecca L. Johnson, Science Writer, Sioux Falls, SD

Copyright © 2007 Sundance Newbridge Publishing

Published by
Sundance Newbridge Publishing
33 Boston Post Road West
Suite 440
Marlborough, MA 01752
800-343-8204
SundanceNewbridge.com

Illustrations by Dan Grant

ISBN: 978-1-4207-0334-4

Printed by Nordica International Ltd
Manufactured in Guangzhou, China
November, 2019
Nordica Job#: CA21901942
SunNew PO#: 229424

Table of Contents

Chapter 1

An Uncertain HONOR

Principal Prescott delivered the news during the end-of-day announcements. "Congratulations to Luis Hernandez," she said. "He has just been named chief science editor for the district's school newspaper."

Luis slumped lower in his seat. It was supposed to be an honor. But Luis wasn't feeling very lucky. He knew what would probably happen next.

Right on cue, Brad Humphrey whispered loudly across the room, "Hey Luis, congratulations! Looks like you're now the head geek of the whole school district."

Luis heard the other kids laugh, but he didn't

look up. He was waiting for the bell to ring. It would rescue him from his misery.

When the bell went off, most kids moved quickly into the hall, but Luis hung back in the classroom. His teacher, Mr. Daniels, looked at him with a raised eyebrow.

"Don't tell me you're going to let that comment from Brad get you down," he challenged.

Luis hung his head. "I know I shouldn't care about guys like Humphrey," he answered. "But he's one of the cool kids, Mr. Daniels. Besides, I just don't know how I got myself into this. I love science, but it's not my whole life. And now I'm responsible for coming up with a science article every three weeks for the paper. All of the parents and kids in the school district will read it, and my name will be on it. Brad Humphrey will have new ammunition on a regular basis."

"Come on, Luis," said Mr. Daniels. "It's not that bad."

"Are you kidding, Mr. Daniels?" asked Luis with growing anxiety. "The other kids who have been assigned to help me include the science fair winners from all of the other schools. I'm sure half the text messages flying around school right now are loaded with 'brainiac' jokes."

Mr. Daniels chuckled. "Luis, you're getting yourself all worked up about the situation before you've even started. Look, you've earned a great opportunity here. Why not just give it a try?"

"Yeah, right," said Luis almost under his breath. Then he gave a small sigh and said a bit louder, "Thanks, Mr. Daniels. I'd better get going,

or I'll be late for my first staff meeting."

As Luis headed for the cafeteria, he thought about how his new honor had come about. Unlike Brad Humphrey, Luis actually enjoyed science. He particularly liked science fair projects. This year he had won top honors with his solar power project. That's what had brought him to the attention of the school superintendent.

One of the superintendent's new projects was a district-wide newspaper. She felt that kids working together from other schools would bring a new sense of community to the district. She had been looking for a science editor, so she interviewed all the science fair winners at each school. Luis turned out to be her top pick. For a moment, Luis allowed himself to feel pleased. After all, the competition had been pretty tough. Maybe Mr. Daniels was right. This could turn out to be a good thing.

Luis entered the cafeteria with new energy. Mrs. Prescott was waiting for him there with the three kids who would make up the staff.

"Everyone," Mrs. Prescott said, "this is Luis, your chief science editor."

A girl with straight black hair stuck her hand out. "Hi, I'm Akane, and I go to Westwood," she said. Before Luis could answer, she went on. "Congratulations on the editor thing. I was the chief science editor at my old school. It was really a lot of work. So I'm really glad I didn't get the job here. You have no idea what you're in for . . . oh, and this is Aaron. He's from Calloway. The only thing he talks about is space. I'm serious, if it doesn't have to do with something 'out there,' he doesn't want to hear it. By the way, when is our first story due? And have you decided what it should be about?"

Akane finally had to stop for a breath. Luis turned to Aaron as quickly as he could.

Aaron eyed Luis. "Do you know anything about space?" he asked.

Luis started to say, "A little, but . . ."

Aaron interrupted. "Never mind—you don't have to. I'm the expert in that subject, and it's the only thing I plan to write about."

Luis couldn't tell if Aaron was kidding or not, so he moved on toward the final member of the team. She was bent over her laptop—popping her gum very loudly. Luis wondered if he should tell her they weren't allowed to chew gum at his school.

Surprisingly Mrs. Prescott overlooked the rule violation. "This is Emily from Eastpoint," she said.

"Yeah, and she hasn't stopped typing on

that keyboard since she walked into the room,"
said Aaron. "Are you playing a video game or
something, Emily?"

"No, I'm looking at some photos of Mars,"
Emily answered with annoyance.

Aaron rolled his eyes in disbelief. He moved
closer and took a peek over her shoulder. "Hey,
she's serious," he said after a moment.

"I'm always serious," answered Emily. "But the
wireless connection is really spotty in here," she
complained. "I vote we meet at my school next
time, Mr. Editor-in-Chief."

It took Luis a moment to understand that she was talking to him. Luis looked at Mrs. Prescott with wide eyes.

She winked at him. "Luis, I think I'll turn this meeting over to you. Remember, you'll have your first science article due to the district office within three weeks. I'll be back in half an hour to see if there are any questions," she said. Then she walked out the door.

Luis looked around the table at the rest of the staff. The room was suddenly very quiet. They were all staring at him. Brad Humphrey's comment about "head geek" suddenly rang loudly in Luis's head. He tried to think of where he should begin. But his mind was blank. He couldn't think of a single thing to say.

Chapter 2

A Shaky START

Akane immediately jumped in. "Luis," she said, "I recommend that you first collect everyone's e-mail address. Then you'll need to make a schedule. And of course we have to discuss the first story. Do we get to vote on the topic? Or are you going to dictate the topic?"

"He is certainly *not* going to dictate the topic," Emily stated flatly. She didn't look up from her computer even for a second.

"Well, he could if he wanted to," argued Akane. "He is head of this staff, you know."

"Yeah," said Aaron. "But if he did something stupid like that, he wouldn't have a staff for long."

Luis couldn't believe it. His staff was already arguing, and he hadn't even said a word.

"Just wait a minute," said Luis finding his voice. "We're supposed to work as a team. So we'll decide on the topic of our first article together."

Emily glanced up for the first time. She gave a small nod of satisfaction. Akane fired off a whole new round of questions. "So what should we write about?" she asked. "Science covers so much. Would you like to write about viruses? Or how about covering an active volcano? Do you want to do a story about amusement park physics? Or should we write about global warming?"

"I already told you," said Aaron. "Space has got to be the topic. It's the only thing worth writing about."

Akane immediately began to disagree. Even Emily, who was obviously interested in space, spoke up about Aaron's limited point of view.

Everyone was talking at once. Luis couldn't make sense of anything they were saying.

"One at a time!" pleaded Luis. But the others kept talking. Luis picked up a textbook. He paused, but just for a moment. Then, in desperation, he slammed the book loudly onto the floor. "QUIET!" he shouted in a stern voice.

Everyone looked at him in surprise. He finally had their attention.

"Look Aaron," Luis said. "We're supposed to be science reporters—by definition that includes a little more than space."

"Fine," said Aaron. "I'll write about space. You write about all of the other stuff."

Luis was amazed at Aaron's single-mindedness. He didn't know whether to be mad or impressed. Finally he said, "Look, I don't necessarily agree with everything Aaron just said. But I do think that space is just as good a subject to start with as any. So why don't we use it for our first article?"

Emily and Akane shrugged their shoulders as if to say, "Why not?"

"Well that narrows it a little," Akane said. "But there are still hundreds of topics. Should we do something on constellations? Or what about the International Space Station?"

"How about the robotic rovers that were sent to Mars?" Emily asked with a flicker of interest. "The pictures they sent back from that planet are really amazing."

"What's with you and Mars?" asked Aaron.

Emily gave Aaron a hard stare. But before another argument could begin, Luis jumped in.

"Mrs. Prescott told me we should think about our audience. What do they already know—and how can we build on that with an interesting story?" he asked.

"Well, let's see," said Akane. "Most everybody knows that the sun is the source of our energy here on Earth. We could do a story about how plants convert light energy into food energy."

"You've GOT to be kidding," said Emily with alarm as she closed her laptop.

Akane paused—but just for a moment. Then she said, "Well, how about something on the planets then? Everybody knows there are nine planets circling the sun in our solar system."

"Not anymore," interrupted Aaron.

"What?" asked Luis.

"I said 'not anymore,'" repeated Aaron.

"What do you mean?" asked Akane. "Even little kids can recite the nine planets: Mercury, Venus, Earth, Mars, Jupiter, Saturn, Uranus, Neptune, and Pluto. Mercury is the planet closest to the sun. Pluto is the planet farthest from the sun."

"No, it's not," said Aaron with a small grin on his face. Akane started to look flustered.

Luis wondered if Aaron was purposely trying to start another argument. He seemed to enjoy annoying people. "What are you saying, Aaron?" he quickly asked.

"I'm saying that there are only eight planets in the solar system. Pluto is no longer a planet," he answered.

"You know, he's actually right on this one," said Emily with a loud snap of her gum. "I read that astronomers from around the world got together and decided to demote Pluto."

"Well, if it's not a planet, then what is it?" asked Akane curiously.

"A big ball of ice—more like a comet than a planet," answered Aaron. "The astronomers decided that Pluto is too small and too different from the other eight to be considered a planet. It's now called a dwarf planet. The whole thing started when an astronomer in California discovered an object much like Pluto—only bigger. And guess what? This thing has its own moon, too."

"Well, why wasn't that new object just added

to the planet list then?" asked Luis.

"It's not that simple," Emily chimed in. "There are lots of new planet-like objects being discovered. So astronomers had to decide on the exact definition of a planet. Now they say that a planet has to orbit the sun and have a round shape."

"But Pluto is round and orbits the sun," interrupted Luis.

"Yeah, but a classical planet, as they're now calling the eight planets in our solar system, has to be big enough to push other objects out of its orbit," Emily continued. "That's where Pluto comes up short. It's a pretty interesting story. In fact, it's almost as interesting as what we're finding out about Mars."

Aaron rolled his eyes, but Akane supported Emily. "I agree. The pictures that have come in from Mars in recent years have really been terrific. I think our readers would be interested to learn how we're continuing to explore our solar system."

"Come on!" protested Aaron. "This is huge! The decision to kick Pluto out of the planet line-up is a much better story."

All three kids turned to look at Luis. They were waiting for him to decide. Luis squirmed in discomfort. Once again he wondered how he had gotten himself into this position. This was not going to be an easy group to work with.

Finally he spoke. "Aaron," Luis began, "the group went along with you in agreeing that the first story should be about space. So now I think we should give the girls a chance. Let's figure out if we can write a good story about how we explore things in our solar system. Then maybe we can follow up with the story about Pluto in another edition."

Akane and Emily nodded their heads in agreement. Aaron thought about it for a moment, then finally nodded as well. Just then Mrs. Prescott came back into the room.

"How did everything go?" she asked with a smile.

Luis answered, "Pretty well. We want to do our first story on the different ways scientists are now gathering information about space. But we're probably going to need some expert advice. What do you think about taking a road trip to the planetarium?"

Emily, Akane, and Aaron looked at Luis. They seemed pleasantly surprised with his idea.

Mrs. Prescott smiled. She seemed a little relieved. "Y'know," she said, "I do know a Dr. Anderson over at the planetarium who is very knowledgeable about space exploration."

Luis, Aaron, Emily, and Akane nodded eagerly at her suggestion. "So when would you like to go?" she asked.

Everyone answered at the same time. "Tomorrow," they all said.

Luis cracked a small smile. It was the first time the whole group had agreed to something without a long debate. Maybe there was hope for his team after all.

Chapter 3

Onward and UPWARD

Mrs. Prescott arranged for Luis and his staff to have a private tour of the planetarium the very next day. The building was right in the middle of the city, and everyone could easily reach it by bus. They all agreed to meet right after school. Since the planetarium closed at 5:30 P.M., they would only have a couple of hours to explore it.

When Luis arrived, the rest of the kids were waiting for him in the lobby. Luis wondered why he was always the last one to show up for their meetings. He asked if he was late.

"No, you're not really late," answered Akane. "But you could've been if the bus was off schedule.

How much time did you allow for error on that? I usually give it about fifteen minutes. But then I also have a built-in cushion. I always set my watch ten minutes ahead."

Luis grinned. "You're kidding. You're that worried about being late?" Luis turned to Emily. "Can you believe she does that?" he asked.

"I think it's a good idea," said Emily. "I do it, too."

Luis looked at Aaron. "Don't tell me . . ."

Aaron nodded yes. Then he said, "But I only set mine eight minutes ahead."

Luis tried to stifle a laugh. "C'mon you guys, you've got to lighten up a little," he said.

"Yeah, either that or maybe you've got to get with the program," challenged Aaron.

Thankfully, the planetarium guide showed up to interrupt the conversation. "My name is Pam," she said. "And I'd like to welcome you to the planetarium. The first thing we have planned today is to take a brief tour of the exhibits. Then I'll take you behind the scenes so that you can talk to Dr. Anderson, who directs all of our education programs here."

The kids eagerly followed Pam into the first exhibit area. It was a display that told the story of the early days of space exploration. Aaron was particularly interested in the 1960s. It was during this time that scientists in the United States were challenged to land a man on the moon. Aaron was fascinated with the early test flights.

"Did you know," Aaron lectured, "that at the very beginning of space exploration, monkeys and chimps were rocketed high in the sky? Eventually

military pilots took a turn. Then in 1962, John Glenn became the first U.S. astronaut to actually orbit Earth. His flight lasted less than five hours, but it paved the way for great things." Emily and Akane looked at each other. But Aaron just continued, "The historic moon landing in July of 1969 would not have been possible without all of those early years of flight tests and experiments."

Aaron's voice trailed off as he wandered through the exhibit. He decided to stay at the space history exhibit while the rest of the group moved on. "I'll meet you out front at closing time," he said.

Luis, Emily, and Akane followed Pam into a long room that housed a display of the solar system. Huge photos and models of the eight planets were hanging from the ceiling.

"Look, Pluto isn't up there with the rest of the planets," Akane said with a grin.

Luis rubbed his chin as if he were considering an important question. "But maybe Pluto and the other dwarf planets *should* be up there."

Akane and Luis both looked to Emily to see if she would jump into the conversation. But Emily wasn't listening. She was gazing up at the pictures hanging around the model of Mars.

"Look at those photographs!" she said with wonder in her voice. "They show us the surface of a planet that is, on average, 140 million miles away from Earth. And those pictures were sent from the cameras of two small robots. They were named *Opportunity* and *Spirit,* and they were launched in June of 2003. It took them a little over six months to get to Mars. But once they got there, they started roaming around the planet, taking pictures of its surface. In fact, *Opportunity* and *Spirit* are still up there on the surface of that cold, rocky planet."

Luis knew he had just lost another member of the group. He could tell that Emily would want to stay at the Mars exhibit for some time. He wouldn't mind doing the same. But he also knew that

someone had to meet with Dr. Anderson. So he
motioned Akane to follow him and Pam.

The next twenty minutes were a blur of
information about light, gravity, motion, and energy.
At one point, Akane stopped to view a collection of
early telescopes. A little boy looking at the exhibit
asked a question about a shooting star. Luis
groaned. He knew that one question could get
Akane talking for the rest of the afternoon. Just as
Luis had expected, Akane told the little boy that a
shooting star was really a meteor.

"A meteor is a piece of rock that has been

sucked into Earth's atmosphere by gravity," she explained. "As the meteor speeds through the atmosphere, it gets very hot and burns up, leaving a streak of light in the sky. That light is what we see as a shooting star!"

The little boy seemed satisfied with this answer, but Luis knew that Akane wouldn't stop there. Sure enough, she began to talk about meteorites next. She dragged the little kid over to a map. Then she began to point out places where some of the biggest meteors hit Earth. Luis knew that a discussion of comets was bound to be next. He was amazed at how much Akane knew. He was also impressed by how fast she could tell a story. Still, he knew she wouldn't be finished with this audience for some time.

"Luis," said Pam. "I know all this is really interesting, but I'm afraid Dr. Anderson is waiting. We'd better move on."

Pam led Luis through an "Employees Only"

door. At the end of the hall, she turned into a
large office. "Luis, I want to introduce you to
Dr. Anderson," said Pam.

Luis saw a young woman in jeans leaning
against the desk. Her hair was tied back in a
ponytail. She wore a T-shirt that had *Everything
I teach is over my head* written on it.

Luis quickly glanced around the room to see
if anyone else was there. Dr. Anderson noticed
his look and grinned. "We don't all look like
white-haired Albert Einsteins, y'know," she said
with a laugh.

Luis was embarrassed. "I guess I was expecting someone . . . a little older," he admitted sheepishly.

"Oh, don't worry, Luis," Dr. Anderson reassured him. "It happens all the time. It really doesn't bother me. I've been a science nerd all my life, so I learned at an early age not to worry about what people think."

"You . . . were a science nerd?" asked Luis.

"Sure I was. Kids used to pick on me all the time in school!" laughed Dr. Anderson. "But I didn't care. I always found math and science more interesting than whatever the bullies were talking about. And now I have the best job in the world because of it."

Luis looked at Dr. Anderson with new respect. Suddenly, Brad Humphrey didn't seem quite so cool.

Chapter 4

Getting with the PROGRAM

"So I hear you're a science reporter," Dr. Anderson said. "How can I help?"

Luis spent the next ten minutes explaining his new role to Dr. Anderson. He told her about the team's struggle to decide on a topic. He finished by asking her if he could interview her about how new information was being gathered about space.

Dr. Anderson said, "Sure, I can tell you about some new projects. But instead of just hearing about space data, how would you and your team like to gather some yourself?"

Luis gave Dr. Anderson a puzzled look. "I'm not quite following you, Dr. Anderson," he said.

"NASA is very committed to educating young people," she said. "So they've set up programs for young people your age. You can actually participate in space exploration."

"They're sending kids my age into outer space?" Luis asked in astonishment.

"Not quite," laughed Dr. Anderson. "But it's the next best thing. NASA has some programs that allow kids to use their own computers to work with scientists in collecting and analyzing data from outer space."

"Are you kidding?" asked Luis.

"It's true," said Dr. Anderson. "In fact, I'm due

to start up a couple of new sessions this month. I'm usually a leader for student groups around here. How would you and your team like to work with me on Saturdays for a while, to see if we can collect some real data about space?"

Luis could hardly believe what he was hearing. Dr. Anderson was inviting them to work with her at the planetarium. At that moment, he was really glad he had listened to Mr. Daniels about giving this new job a chance.

"There are actually a couple of programs you can participate in," continued Dr. Anderson. "The first one allows us to take a special look at Mars. Our team will get to pick a real site on Mars for study. Then a special camera that is on a spacecraft currently orbiting Mars will shoot images of that site. The images will be sent over the Internet to our computer here at the planetarium. Then we'll use special image processing tools to help us enhance the pictures for our study. We'll analyze what we

have and can then talk about our results with real experts at NASA."

"So the research is real and so are the results?" asked Luis.

"You got it, Luis," answered Dr. Anderson.

"Emily, one of the girls in our group, would absolutely love to do that," he said. "She's got this thing about Mars."

"There's another project you also might be interested in," continued Dr. Anderson. "In this case, we would get to 'borrow' the use of a really big radio telescope that is out in the desert. We can actually control the telescope through our own computer here. Then we can collect real data and use a computer software program to help us analyze it. Again we report our results to real

scientists who might find the data useful."

"I would really like to try that," said Luis in amazement. "So what time should we be here on Saturday?" he asked.

"Well, first you need to clear it with your parents," Dr. Anderson said. "But if they agree, then I think 10:00 A.M. would be fine. However, right now you need to go find the rest of your group," she said looking at her watch. "It's almost 5:30, and the planetarium will be closing very soon."

Luis thanked Dr. Anderson again and retraced his steps toward the telescopes. He expected to find Akane there—still talking, of course. But when he got to the exhibit where he left her, he was surprised to find the room empty.

Akane must have headed back toward the solar system display to meet Emily, Luis thought. So he headed that way. Unfortunately Luis didn't find anyone when he got there, either.

Luis looked around for a few minutes. It was

really nice when it wasn't so crowded. He spent some more time reading the signs along the walls.

After a while, Luis decided he'd better get going. So he headed toward the space history display. Surely Aaron would still be there. But he wasn't. Neither was anyone else.

Luis was a bit annoyed. He couldn't believe his team would just leave him. He wanted to tell them the good news about working with Dr. Anderson. But it would serve them right if they didn't hear about it until tomorrow, he decided.

Luis moved in the direction of the lobby, but as he passed a restroom, he decided he'd better stop in. After all, it might be a long ride home on the bus during rush hour traffic. He smiled to himself as he wondered how much time Akane had built into her schedule for the trip home. He couldn't believe his whole team set their watches ahead. He wondered why they had ever started doing that.

As he entered the bathroom, Luis realized that

while he was daydreaming he had just missed an announcement being made over the loudspeaker. "Oh well," he said to himself. "If it's important they'll repeat it."

When Luis came out of the restroom, he was suddenly aware that the planetarium looked different. The lights had been dimmed. Luis felt a sudden wave of nervousness. He glanced at his watch. Then he did a double take. Luis sucked in a big breath of air. It was 5:45 P.M.!

Luis started to run toward the lobby. When he reached it, his sneakers made a loud squeak on the marble floor as he pulled up short. Luis couldn't believe what he was seeing. The doors had a big bar across them. The planetarium was closed—and he was locked inside!

Chapter 5

A Confusing TIME

Luis wasn't the only one to figure this out. Three faces were pressed against the outside of the glass door looking in. Akane smiled and waved when she saw him. Emily shook her head in disbelief. Aaron just pointed to his watch as if to tell Luis he should've gotten with the program.

Luis was in a panic. What was he going to do? He looked around for a security guard to let him out. There wasn't a single person in sight. He looked at his team for help.

Aaron just rolled his eyes and flipped open his cell phone. Good idea, thought Luis as he pulled his phone from his pocket. But he realized he didn't know Aaron's number. Luckily Aaron was a step ahead of him. He was holding up a piece of paper. Luis squinted through the glass to read the numbers and quickly punched them in.

"Way to go, Chiefy," said Aaron when he answered Luis's phone call.

"Aaron, what do I do?" asked Luis breathlessly. "I've got to get out of here before I get in big trouble."

"You're right about that first part. But I think it's maybe too late for the second part," Aaron answered. "Look behind you."

Luis swung around. A security guard was

walking toward him. Luis thought he looked very big. He also thought he looked very annoyed.

"What are you doing in here, kid?" the guard asked. "Don't you know we're closed?"

"Well sir, it seems I accidentally got locked in," Luis stammered.

"How could that happen?" asked the guard. "Didn't you hear the announcement about closing? Now take that backpack off and slide it toward me. Then I want you to take everything out of your pockets slowly."

Luis carefully did what he was told. The guard looked everything over. When he was satisfied that Luis wasn't stealing anything and had no weapon, he motioned him to follow.

"Now we've got to go back to the office. I'm going to have to file a report on all this," he said with a sigh. "And then we're going to have to call your parents. But first," he continued, "you need to call your little friends out there and tell them the show's over. It's time for them to go home. And have them back off that window right now—they're leaving nose smudges all over the glass!"

Luis redialed Aaron's number and relayed the message. Aaron couldn't say too much. He was laughing too hard at what Luis had just said.

The next day in school was a real treat. Luis couldn't believe how fast word had spread. Brad Humphrey was the first to come up to Luis in the hall.

"Hey man, I think maybe I had you all wrong," he teased. "I don't think you should worry about being King of the Nerds anymore, Luis. I mean, you're not exactly a rocket scientist if you can't get out of a public building before it closes," he finished with a laugh. Then he slapped Luis on the back and moved on down the hall.

"Doesn't look like we need a district newspaper to me," Luis grumbled. "It seems news spreads pretty fast around here without one."

Luis was feeling very confused. Yesterday he had been worried about being labeled a science nerd. Then he had been proud that he was going to work with Dr. Anderson. But today he was the topic of everyone's jokes because of a stupid mistake he had made. Luis wondered which kid he really was.

An after-school meeting was scheduled with Mrs. Prescott and the team. Luis arrived 20 minutes early. Mrs. Prescott asked about the mishap at the planetarium. Luis explained it was an accident.

Mrs. Prescott said she understood, but she asked him to pay more attention in the future.

Aaron and Akane arrived together. "Hey, look at this, Akane," Aaron teased. "The Chief is here early today! Guess his brush with the law made him get with the program," he said as he pointed to his watch.

"Just ignore Aaron," Akane reassured Luis. "We're just glad you're alright. Although it was kind of funny to see your face when you realized you were locked in. But we were glad you were able to get out so quickly. By the way, Mrs. Prescott said you had big news. Did you get to see Dr. Anderson? Is there anything new on the article?"

"Give him a chance to answer why don't you?" grumbled Emily as she walked in. As usual, her laptop was securely in place under her arm.

Mrs. Prescott started the meeting. "We have some very big news for all of you. Dr. Anderson from the planetarium has invited you to work with her on some special projects. Believe it or not, you will actually be collecting real data from outer space."

Everyone looked at Luis. He grinned at their wide-eyed expressions. "Yep, it's true . . . and Dr. Anderson is really cool," he said. Then he told them all about the two projects and their invitations to work at the planetarium on Saturdays.

Emily was the first to speak. "Luis, I admit I wasn't sure about you at the beginning. But you keep surprising me. I can't believe we get to work with new data from Mars! It will be the coolest thing I've ever done. Count me in. Where do I go? When do I start?"

"You're starting to sound like Akane," Aaron said. He thought Akane would protest, but she didn't say a thing. Aaron continued, "I agree. This sounds like a sweet deal. Count me in."

Everyone looked at Akane for her reaction. They expected her to be bubbling over with questions. But Akane was just staring down at her desk. Finally she raised her head to speak.

"I agree it's a great opportunity," she said. "But I just can't do it."

"Of course you can," said Luis. "You can't study all the time, Akane. Take some time off to have some fun with us! I told you, you have to lighten up a little."

"It's not that, Luis," said Akane in a quivering voice. The others were shocked to see tears welling

up in her eyes.

"What is it, Akane?" asked Mrs. Prescott.

"It's my mom. She's sick, and I have to take care of her on Saturdays while my dad works," she replied. "I can't possibly leave her to go to the planetarium." Then she jumped up and ran out of the room.

No one said anything. Luis felt terrible. He knew he had only been worrying about himself for the last few days. It had never even occurred to him to find out more about his own staff. He now realized that Akane's troubles made his own look very small.

A Real Team EFFORT

On Saturday morning, Luis, Aaron, and Emily met again at the planetarium. They were all silent for a moment as they thought about Akane. Then Luis looked at Emily more closely.

"Hey, wait a minute," he said. "Something's different about you."

"What?" asked Emily with a sly grin. "C'mon, let's get in there and see Dr. Anderson."

"No, Chiefy's right," said Aaron. "There is something different about you today."

"I've got it!" exclaimed Luis. "You don't have your laptop. What happened? Did you get a virus or something?"

"No, I just don't have it today," shrugged Emily. "No big deal."

"No big deal?" echoed Aaron. "It's like you forgot to wear clothes or something, Emily! That thing's always attached to you."

"What?" asked Emily in annoyance. "C'mon, if we're late, we're going to get stuck with the crummy seats."

The boys followed Emily down the hall. Luis wondered why Emily was trying so hard to change the subject. But he knew there was no sense in pushing her. If Emily didn't want to talk about something—she didn't talk about it.

When they reached the computer lab, Dr. Anderson greeted them warmly. There were other students about their age in the room. There were also a few graduate students whom Dr. Anderson had invited in to help.

"We're going to form two teams," explained Dr. Anderson. "One team will work on the Mars study group. The other will be assigned to the radio telescope project. Does anyone have a strong preference for what team they'd like to work on?"

Nobody cared except Emily. She raised her hand and said, "I would really like to work on the Mars team." Luis and Aaron weren't surprised.

Dr. Anderson quickly separated them into their groups and began to explain their assignments. Luis was overwhelmed. As he sat down and looked at the row of computers in front of him, he felt like he was at the Kennedy Space Center working on a real launch. He could tell by looking at Aaron and Emily that they were thinking the same thing. The only thing that made him feel bad was that Akane was not there to experience it, too.

The morning flew by. Luis and Aaron worked together on the radio telescope team. They learned that the radio antenna that they would be

"borrowing" was located in California. It was one of several huge radio telescopes built to help scientists stay in constant radio contact with spacecraft flying into deep space. The huge antenna had a dish that was 110 feet wide. The whole thing stood nine stories high.

The real excitement came when the team actually took control of the radio telescope themselves for the first time. They linked through the Internet to the operations center in California. Then the control of the huge deep space antenna was actually in their hands. They programmed their computer to aim the antenna toward the planet Jupiter. Their goal was to measure differences in the radio emissions from Jupiter's radiation belts. Luis and Aaron felt like real scientists as they watched the data roll in.

Emily was also experiencing some out-of-this-world excitement. Her team was looking for just the right spot to get a good image. They wanted to

compare the surface of Mars with areas of known water erosion on Earth. If the markings were similar, it might give scientists a better clue as to whether liquid water once existed in this area on Mars.

Aside from a short break for lunch, the two teams worked all day. They set up schedules and worked on reports. Luis was amazed at the teamwork. Even Aaron, who usually liked to argue so much, gave his full cooperation to the group.

When it was time to leave, Dr. Anderson called Luis, Emily, and Aaron into her office.

"So what did you think?" she asked with a big grin.

Even though they were exhausted, all three kids began talking at once.

"Hold up," laughed Dr. Anderson. "Can you give it to me one at a time?"

Aaron went first. "I got to adjust the aim of the telescope," he said proudly. Luis smiled. Aaron sounded like a little boy who had just learned how to ride a two-wheeled bike for the first time.

Luis wasn't far behind in his enthusiasm. "We saw some real spikes in the radiation emissions," he claimed.

"Hey man," said Aaron. "You sound like a real scientist." Luis beamed at the compliment.

Emily didn't like to beam. But she just couldn't help it. "You should have seen some of the craters we looked at," she said. "Won't it be great if some of our results are actually used someday back in the space lab?"

"I just wish that Akane could've been here," said Luis. "It doesn't seem fair that she missed all this."

Emily and Dr. Anderson exchanged a smile.

"Well, let's see what she thought about it all," said Dr. Anderson as she moved to her computer screen and began to type.

"What are you talking about?" asked Luis. Aaron looked puzzled, too.

Emily looked over Dr. Anderson's shoulder and began to read the screen. "Akane says she really enjoyed looking at all of the Mars images today. She said her mother enjoyed looking at them, too. Oh, and Luis, she wants to remind you that we only have two weeks left before the first article is due for the newsletter."

"What's going on?" asked Luis. "How does Akane know about the images of Mars?"

Aaron slapped himself on the forehead with the

palm of his hand. "NOW I get it!" he burst out. He turned to Emily and smiled.

Luis said, "Will somebody please fill me in?"

Dr. Anderson obliged. "When Akane said she couldn't make it in for the study, Emily called me right away. She wanted to know if there was a way to set Akane up as a remote location to the project. I made a few phone calls and got her added to the list. So when we got an image of Mars today, all we had to do was transfer it to Akane. Then she could look at it along with us. Turns out that all Akane needed was a wireless laptop at her home."

Luis looked at Emily.

"Hey, it's no big deal," she said.

"No, you're wrong, Emily," Luis answered. "It was a big deal—and I think it's cool to be working with you and everyone else on this team."

"Is that a quote, Chiefy?" asked Aaron.

"You bet it is," answered Luis. "And the first person I'm going to tell about this whole thing on

Monday is Brad Humphrey."

"Who's Brad Humphrey?" asked Emily as she started to gather her things to go home.

"Let me tell you about him," said Luis as they waved good-bye to Dr. Anderson and started to walk down the hall. "He's a kid who really used to bug me . . . but I'm over it now."

THE END

Glossary

classical planet a body that orbits the sun, is large enough that its own gravity pulls it into a nearly round shape, and is large enough that it pushes smaller objects out of its orbit

comet a ball of ice and rock that orbits the sun and has a tail of gas and dust

constellation a group of stars that forms a pattern or picture when you "connect the dots" between them

dictate to order someone to do something

dwarf planet a body that orbits the sun and is large enough that its own gravity pulls it into a nearly round shape, but is not large enough to push smaller objects out of its orbit

emissions something put out in the air

meteor a mass of rock that is pulled toward the earth by gravity, and that makes a streak of light in the sky as it burns up while traveling through the atmosphere

meteorite a meteor that has reached the surface of the earth

NASA the National Aeronautics and Space Administration, which runs the U.S. space program

obliged to do something as a favor

radio telescope an instrument that detects and records radio waves coming from stars and other objects in space

solar system a group of planets, asteroids, comets, meteors, and other objects that orbit the sun

star a mass of gases that is held together by its own gravity

telescope an instrument containing lenses and mirrors that enlarges objects that are far away